GOLDIE

NICOLE RUBEL

HARPER & ROW, PUBLISHERS

Library of Congress Cataloging-in-Publication Data

Rubel, Nicole.

  Goldie.

  Summary: A tiny chicken causes big mischief when
she goes shopping with her mother.

  [1. Shopping—Fiction. 2. Chickens—Fiction]

I. Title.

PZ7.R828Go 1989   [E]   88-32796

ISBN 0-06-025096-8

ISBN 0-06-025097-6 (lib. bdg.)

To my husband Richard

"Goldie, help me choose a dress for the dance tonight," said Mom.

"Do you like this one? I'm going to try it on."

"It's too small! Stay here in the dressing room while I find a larger size."

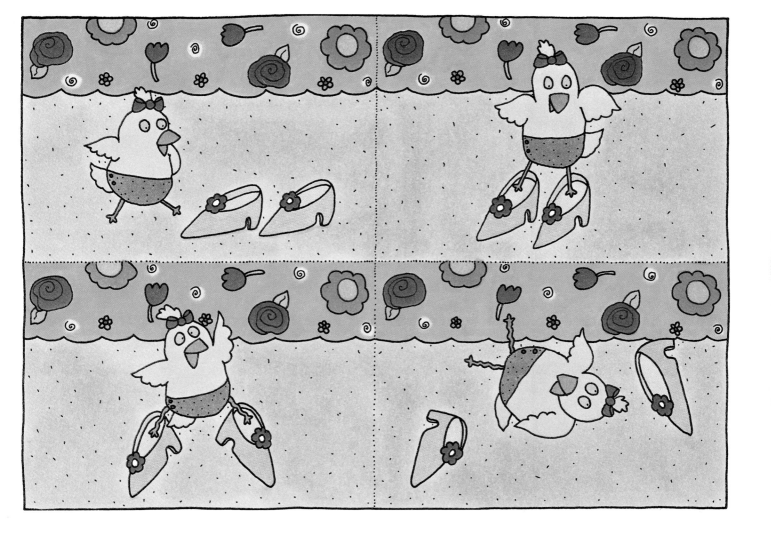

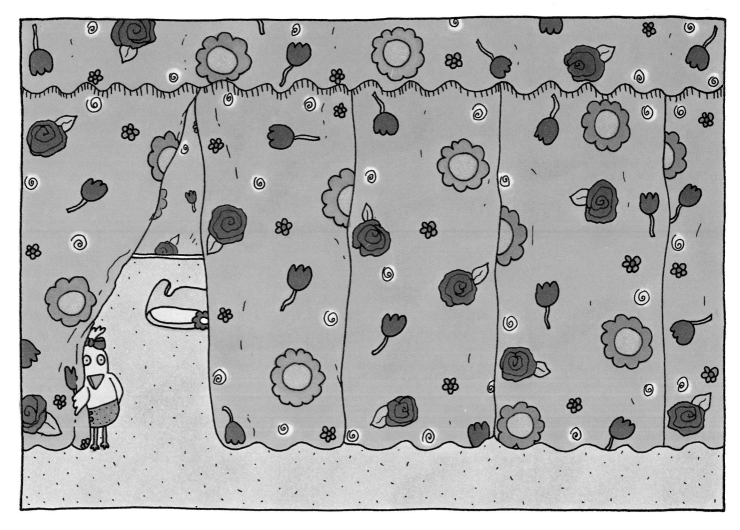

But Goldie didn't want to stay in the dressing room.

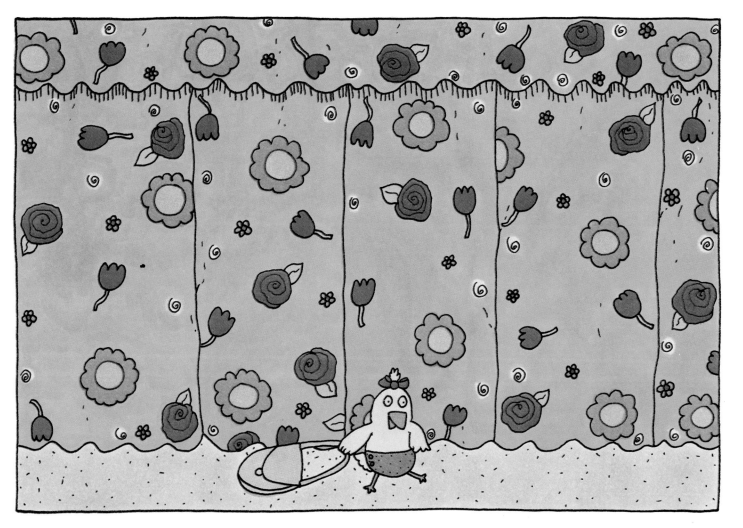

She wanted to go shopping too.

"Hello, that's a nice dress you're wearing," she said to
the first shopper she met. But the shopper didn't answer.

"Goldie!" cried Mom, rushing over.

Back in the dressing room, Goldie promised to sit still.
"I'll be back in a minute," said Mom. "I'm just going to buy this dress."

"My goodness!" meowed the cat.

"Oh, my!" cried the kangaroo, jumping high into the air.

"Good gracious!" trumpeted the elephant, and they all ran away.

"Goldie!" cried Mom. "*Here* I am.

"I bought the dress. Now let's find something nice for you."

"Anything but a hat!" said Goldie.

"Let's buy this pair of sunglasses!" said Goldie.

"It's time to go home," said Mom.

And that night...